CROW TALK

A flock of crows gets nooked on this funny story.

Kathy Henderson is an artist and illustrator, as well as an author. She has written many picture books for children, including *In the Middle of the Night*, *The Year in the City*, *The Baby Dances*, *The Storm* (which was shortlisted for the Kate Greenaway Medal) and *The Little Boat*, Winner of the Kurt Maschler Award and shortlisted for the Smarties Book Prize. She is also the author of the Walker young fiction titles *Second-time Charley*, *Pappy Mashy* and *Jim's Winter*. She has three children and lives in London.

Books by the same author

Pappy Mashy

Jim's Winter

Second-time Charley

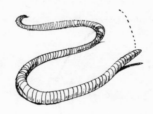

KATHY HENDERSON
Illustrations by
DAVID HUGHES

WALKER BOOKS
AND SUBSIDIARIES
LONDON • BOSTON • SYDNEY

First published 1996 by Walker Books Ltd
87 Vauxhall Walk, London SE11 5HJ

This edition published 2001

2 4 6 8 10 9 7 5 3 1

Text © 1996 Kathy Henderson
Illustrations © 1996 David Hughes

This book has been typeset in Plantin

Printed and bound in Great Britain
by the Guernsey Press Co. Ltd

British Library Cataloguing in Publication Data:
a catalogue record for this book is
available from the British Library

ISBN 0-7445-8247-4

Contents

Chapter 1

Scum Makes a Discovery

....

Scum the crow was late for the Evening Caw.

"Stinking November," muttered the young bird as he flew across the city towards the park.

It was raining. The roads were greasy. The roofs were slippery. The wind was whipping the last leaves off the few trees that weren't already as bare as lamp posts.

"Slime and garbage!" croaked Scum. "This is no fun!" and he flopped down on the TV aerial of 23 Blount Street with a thump.

"My claws are cold. I'm starving hungry. There isn't a squashed rat or a mouldy apple in sight and it's two days before the dustmen come and spill rubbish all over the road again. I don't care about the Evening Caw!

Boring. That's what it is. Always the same caw, caw, caw, in the top of the trees.

Boring, boring, cawing's boring,
Boring, boring, cawing's boring.
I want a change!"

There was another thump. Leatherlegs, one of his thirty-seven older brothers and sisters, landed beside him. The aerial rocked.

"Move over. Move over!" cawed Leatherlegs.

"Move over yourself!" Scum hung on tighter.

"Caw. This wind doesn't half get up your tail feathers. Caw. Caw. And we'd better hurry or we'll be late!"

"So what?"

"What did you say?" Leatherlegs was so surprised he almost fell off his perch.

"I said so what?" Scum stretched himself, "I'm not going."

"But what about the others? Everyone *always* comes back in the evening!"

"Yes, but why? Why shouldn't I do something different for a change?"

This was a bit much for Leatherlegs.

Thinking was not his strong point.

"Because ... Well ... Because birds of a feather stick together!"

"Yawk!"

Scum settled himself firmly over the joint of the TV aerial, gripped it hard with his claws and shut his eyes.

"I'm not budging," he said.

"Oh, dear me," muttered Leatherlegs and, losing his balance, he flopped down on to the chimney pot.

The aerial lurched. The rain ran down Scum's shiny black feathers and trickled under his claws. He hung on tighter. Then something strange happened.

His toes started to tingle.

His feathers started to fizz.

And in front of his eyes, his tightly closed eyes, in glorious summer-sunshine colour he saw ...

pictures,

moving pictures,

pictures of food!

Scum's beak fell open.

"OOOOARK!" he gasped, keeping his eyes tight shut.

Leatherlegs put his head on one side and looked up at him.

"You look funny," he said. "Your feathers are standing on end."

Scum didn't answer. Instead he started to sing in a faint voice, not like his own at all:

"*Skitty Kitty's full of meat*
Chunky mush cats love to eat."

"Cats?" cawed Leatherlegs, amazed.

"*Give some to your skitty kitty today,*" cooed Scum.

"But no crow sings about cats!"

Leatherlegs hopped from foot to foot in alarm. But Scum took no notice: he had started on another song.

"*Crunchburgers,*" he crooned,
"*Lunchburgers.*
Greasy, grimy, slippery, slimy, Munchburgers."

"He must be going mad!" cawed Leatherlegs to the wind. "He must be going out of his tiny feathers! Oh dear, oh dear! What am I going to do? And all because he wouldn't go to the Evening Caw!"

Scum's voice changed yet again.

"*And now for the weather forecast*," he announced.

This was definitely too much for Leatherlegs. He jumped back up on to the aerial and butted him hard with his head.

"Scum! Scum!" he shouted. "Wake up!"

Scum opened his eyes, lost his grip and fell off his perch.

"What d'you want to do that for?" he squawked. "I was enjoying myself!"

Down in the front room of 23 Blount Street Mrs Hetty Cox was fiddling with the controls of her television set.

"I don't know what's the matter with the thing," she said to her blue budgerigar, Timmy, who was hopping around in his cage impatiently.

"One minute it's all fizzles and flashes. The

next minute the pictures go all wobbly and now it's all right again. I'll have to get my Bernard to do something about it next time he pops in."

Timmy whistled sympathetically.

Chapter 2

The Gathering

That evening, Scum's mother and father, his brothers and sisters, cousins and aunts and uncles and grandparents and great aunts and great uncles and all their friends and relatives gathered round in the top of the trees in the park. Their shiny black feathers gleamed in the rain, their bright eyes glittered and the air rang with their cawing long after the usual time. The extraordinary lateness of Scum and Leatherlegs and the strange tale they brought with them when they finally reached the roost had every beak wagging.

"It's true!" shrugged Scum, standing on a branch in the middle of the assembled crows. "It's as true as I'm perching here. I could see them, hear them, like in a sort of dream. Pictures in my head. Pictures of food. Songs they were singing. Sort of visions."

"Visions? Visions indeed!" clucked Scum's stout aunt Squawk. "What kind of crow has visions with *cats* in them?"

"Missing the Evening Caw too," grumbled an old crow called Doom.

"Caw! Caw!" added his brother Gloom. "I don't know what's happening to the youth of today."

"No respect for tradition," grumbled Smog, another of the older birds.

"In my young day…" cawed Gloom.

"Well I saw it and I heard it. And that's what it said," insisted Scum and he started to whistle "Skitty Kitty's full of meat" for the twentieth time. "It's still better than just singing caw, caw, caw, all the time." Scum lifted his head and looked defiantly at the others. "I don't know about you, but I'm cold and I'm hungry and I'm fed up with sitting in these trees every night doing nothing. At least what I saw makes a change. So as soon as morning comes I'm going back to see some more."

"Change!"

"New?"

"Going off on his own?"

"Did you ever hear such nonsense!"

It seemed as if every bird there was cawing its disapproval.

Scum shrugged and closed his eyes. Then he heard a different noise overhead. He opened his eyes again and saw Rummage, his third cousin twice·removed, grinning at him and turning somersaults on a wet branch.

"*My mate Scum is off his head*," she sang to no one in particular.

"*Won't sing caw, sings miaow instead.*"

Scum had had enough. With a loud screech he flew at her, pushed her off her branch and fell wrestling and tumbling through the air to the bushes below.

The crow crowd screeched and cawed and flapped their wings.

"What's the world coming to? Caw! Caw! Caw!"

Now a very large crow stood up on his perch and beat his shiny wings for silence.

It was Rawk, their leader.

"It seems to me," he said slowly when the noise had subsided, "that the youngster deserves a hearing. Leaving aside the question of missing the Evening Caw," he stared sternly down his beak at Scum, "he may have discovered something. However much we value our traditions, we should not turn our backs on the new without investigating first. He talks of visions. He sings new caws. He speaks of food." Rawk's eyes gleamed greedily. "Rather than letting one of our young stray from the flock, I propose that we send a group of senior crows to look into the matter in the morning." He swivelled his head and looked round at them all. "And so goodnight to you all."

The meeting was over.

Well knock me down with a feather! thought Scum to himself as he drifted off to sleep. Fancy old Rawk almost believing me.

Chapter 3

Caw, Look at That!

....

The next morning Scum and Leatherlegs led
Doom and Gloom and Soot and Smog and a
small group of other older crows over the
rooftops to 23 Blount Street. Scum pointed
out the aerial.

"That?!"

"We all know those things!"

"There are thousands of them. We've been
sitting on them for years. Messages? Visions?"
The old crows cackled and laughed.

Gloom held up his wing, "Well?" he said
sceptically.

Scum hopped up on to the centre joint of
the aerial, closed his eyes, hung on tightly
with his claws and wobbled the loose aerial
about a bit.

Within seconds his feathers started to
ruffle.

"I've got it!" he cawed.

"And what exactly have you got?" asked Gloom.

Scum's voice changed. "…*Today*," he intoned, "*I'll be showing you how to make rich beef casserole with button mushrooms in a pastry shell,*"

"Food! Food! He's got food!" cawed the other crows.

"*followed by Grandma Robinson's treacle pudding with raspberry sauce.*"

"Where is it?"

"Let's see!"

"Food! Food! Food!"

All the old crows, except for Doom, were mad with curiosity now. They jumped up on to the aerial. They crowded closer. They jammed up against Scum and squeezed and pressed.

"Close your eyes," squeaked Scum, nearly squashed to porridge.

"Caaaaaw!" they all said at once, eyes tightly closed. "Caw, look at that!"

Doom sat apart on the chimney pot.

"That's not food," he croaked in his gravelly old voice, "not real food anyway. It's just television. My grandma knew all about television. *She* used to have a special arrangement with the bin men at the television building... Now that *was* food! Trucks full of it! Convoys of them! You should have heard her stories!" But nobody was listening to him.

Downstairs Mrs Cox was doing her ironing in front of the television as usual. The picture fizzed. The sound crackled.

"I don't know," she said to her battle-scarred old cat Fluffikins. "The reception on this set seems to get worse every day."

Fluffikins snoozed.

"Cookery Challenge" came sizzling to an end. The ads burbled and fizzed and then "Cat Lovers Weekly" began. Suddenly the picture cleared.

Above Blount Street a group of cawing, tumbling crows were speeding back towards the roost as fast as they could go.

* * *

"Let me get this clear," said Rawk, bringing the extraordinary midday meeting to order. "As long as you're feather-to-feather with someone else who's touching someone else who's touching the crow in the middle of the aerial, you say you can see these things?"

"Yes! And hear the music."

"You can almost taste the food!"

"As for the jingles:
Crunchy crisps are super-light
Scrunch that crunch in every bite."

"*Smokey bacon!*"

"*Cheese 'n' onion!*"

"*Prawn cocktail!*"

"Order!" called Rawk. "Order! Does this mean that all of us, the entire flock, could watch this? Together?"

"Yeah! Can we?"

"Why not roost there?"

"It's much better than the park!"

"And that food!"

"Why don't we all go?"

"Caw!"

Doom broke in.

"You cannot be serious. You're not proposing that we leave this roost, these trees which have been our home for countless generations?"

"Yes! Yes!"

"And roost instead on the rooftops of the city, on wire trees, among human beings and motorcars and cats? And all for the sake of television?"

"Yeah! Caw! Yeah!"

"Move with the times!"

"Winter's coming. It's boring here."

"Give it a try!"

The elders put their heads together. There was much cawing and chatter and after a while old Doom flew off and sat stiffly on a branch by himself. Finally Rawk emerged.

"We are," he said slowly, smoothing the sleek black feathers that had become a little ruffled in the discussion, "we are prepared to give it a go for a trial period."

The cheers and caws rang through the windswept park.

"There is, however, one condition," said Rawk when the noise had died down. "And that is that I, as your leader, take the central perch on the aerial."

"I might have guessed," sighed Scum.

Mrs Cox's son Bernard came to see her that evening. He was a big man with a red face, spectacles and receding hair.

"Brrr!" he said as he closed the front door and unwound the scarf from round his neck. "Winter's here! And there are a lot of birds around tonight. You should hear the racket they're making. Your roof's full of them."

He took the cup of tea his mother offered him, sat down in the big armchair and picked up the newspaper.

"I think there's something wrong with the television," said Mrs Cox. "It keeps flickering. Sometimes it goes all fuzzy."

"Looks all right to me," said Bernard, not

looking up. "Maybe you have it on too much. You only turn it off when you go to bed."

"Well I don't get out much any more," said Mrs Cox. "It's all I've got for company."

"You've got Fluffikins and the budgie," said Bernard. "And you've got me." He carried on reading.

"Yes, dear. But you will have a look for me, won't you? I do like to watch 'One in a Million' of a Friday night."

"All right," said Bernard, still not looking up from the newspaper. "No. On second thoughts, it sounds like the aerial. I'll give the engineer a call."

Chapter 4

Hooked

The talent contest "One in a Million" was Mrs Cox's favourite programme. Though she had the television on from first thing in the morning till last thing at night, this was the highpoint of her week. Every Friday evening without fail she would stop whatever else she was doing, settle in her armchair with Fluffikins on her knee and watch, fascinated, as the would-be stars of the future trooped across her screen in search of fame and fortune.

Every aspiring comedian and beginner guitarist in the land, every loopy lyric writer and soppy singer longed to appear on the show. They dreamed of stepping on to the sparkling stage of the television studio, taking their place beside Fat Henry, the host of the show, and seizing the attention of the world for two magical minutes. Week by week they struggled to outdo each other, and to win through from their round into the quarter finals, from the quarter finals to the semi finals until, at last, the Grand Final of the competition decided on the winner of all winners: that One in a Million.

Mrs Cox, alone with her cat and her budgerigar, loved every minute of it.

And the crows squatting on her rooftop soon became passionate fans too. They had taken to their new life like ducks to water.

Within hours of arriving, they'd established their roosting places. Rawk sat high in the centre of the aerial like a black statue against the sky. The rest of the flock spread out around him feather-to-feather down across the chimney pots and out across the ridges of the roofs, scores of crows arranged strictly in order of importance.

Before the first day was over they had coated the roof in a slime of bird-droppings that got thicker and thicker as time passed.

Within a week the habits of a thousand generations of crows had started to change. It was as if the world of twigs and trees, nests and scavenging no longer existed.

Where before they had been on the move all day singly or in pairs, hopping and hunting or flying and cawing, now they crowded together to sit still hour after hour, with their eyes tightly shut, drinking in every last minute of Mrs Cox's television choice.

Where all their lives they had gathered to caw at dusk and gone to sleep when darkness fell, now they stayed awake long after dark to sit and watch until Mrs Cox turned her television set off at 11.00 p.m. And instead of waking at dawn to gobble up the first insects of the day, now they only roused themselves, hungry and dopey, when it was already light and "Breakfast Beano" came on.

Their songs changed too. Gone were the cries and caws of crows down the centuries. Now they sang snatches of advertisements about insurance companies and soap powder, fizzy drinks and burgers. And they not only sang them (every fifteen minutes all through the day), they believed them too!

Suddenly the old food was no good. Slugs were out. Beetles were too much hard work. Rubbish and leftovers had lost their charm. Now only *Crunchy Crisps* and *Drooppin Donuts, Skitty Kitty* and *Super Microwave-ready Chicken Chasseur* would do. A few of the more adventurous crows tried raiding loaded trollies in supermarket car parks or plundering the back doors of pubs and restaurants. The rest preferred to sit on the roof and feed on pictures rather than miss an instalment of "Them Next Door" or "Motorway Disaster".

And as for "One in a Million", before a month was out, there wasn't a bird on the rooftop who wouldn't choose to starve or freeze and never fly again rather than miss a single minute of the nation's favourite Friday night spectacular.

They were hooked!

Winter wore on.

The park was deserted. The litter uncollected. The trees empty.

Only old Doom had stayed behind.

"It's the end of crowvilization," he moaned, alone on his perch.

"Nothing good will come of it, you mark my words."

Mrs Cox's Bernard was not pleased either.

"This is getting beyond a joke," he said as he came in one evening in December wiping a bird mess off the top of his head. "There are hundreds of those birds out there. The path's covered in mess. Death trap it is. It's lucky you don't go out there much. And just look at my coat! No. You can't leave it like that. It's a health risk. I'm going to get in touch with the Pest Control Office at the Council on Monday."

Mrs Cox looked at her budgie.

"Don't worry Bernard," she said. "You know I like birds. They give me something to look at. And I'm sure they don't mean any harm really. Eh, Timmy?"

Timmy chirped.

"But I would be ever so grateful if you could do something about the television," she went on. "It's so fuzzy I can hardly see it sometimes. And you know what? It's the oddest thing, but sometimes I think I can see the shadow of wings crossing the screen!"

Bernard looked at his mother and shook his head.

Chapter 5

Time to Fly

....

And what about Scum?

To begin with he was keen as mustard. He flapped around the aerial offering advice to Rawk on viewing positions and improving reception. He drank in every show, every film and every advertisement as if there had never been anything so interesting in the world. He was the first to learn the words of the jingles and was expert on the details of which programmes were on when. But…

As the days went by and the elders of the flock settled into their new life, Scum found that he was no longer welcome up by the aerial. His help wasn't needed. He was pushed down into his own place in the pecking order, 139 birds away from the top in a draughty corner of the roof where his feet got cramped and his wings got squashed and the picture was so bad he could hardly make it out.

Gradually as the weeks came and went, as December stretched into January and January yawned on towards February, as the other crows got less and less interested in anything except television, television, television, and as Mrs Cox's choice of programmes got more and more familiar, so Scum got more and more hungry, fidgety and cross.

The day of the "One in a Million" final was the last straw. Every second programme seemed to be a trailer for the big night, every ad seemed more idiotic than the last. Suddenly Scum had had enough. Pushing his way out of his place in the squash, he straightened out his crumpled feathers, slid down the flank of the roof and stood on the gutter.

"You know what," he cawed hoarsely. "THIS IS *BORING!*"

"Ssssh!" croaked his uncle Scar from a little way up the roof, "We're trying to hear

'Sunset Singalong'."

"If you can't be quiet, caw away and play. Caw."

Scum was indignant.

"Who discovered this anyway?" he screeched up at them. "Did anybody thank me? Did they? Did anybody ask me if I wanted to be 139th in the line? Eh?"

He strutted up and down the gutter's edge jerking his head backwards and forwards and working himself into a fury. But none of the other crows took any notice. They all had their eyes shut. Then Rummage flew down and landed in front of him.

"Caw, I'm stiff," she said, stretching her wings. "If I stay up there much longer, I'll forget how to fly. What's up?"

"What's up?" snapped Scum. "*Nothing's* up. That's the trouble! It's just like it was before. Then it was the same old caw, caw, caw, in the park every day. Now it's television, television, television. We don't even fly any more. I'm stiff. I'm hungry and

I'm bored, bored, BORED."

As he spoke there was a shifting and ruffling above them.

"Silence down there," cawed Scar. "At once!"

"Are you ready?" called Rawk from the aerial top.

Rummage groaned. "Oh no. Not again! Not the blooming advertisements!"

Scum hid his head under his wing.

The mangy crowd of crows on the roof above were rustling and stirring, they were puffing up their once fine chest feathers and clearing their beaks. Then suddenly they all burst into song at once.

"*Soapy Snow's the only one*," they squawked,

"*To get your clothes really clean when the*
washing's done.
It's the last goodbye to grime and dirt
Just a scoop full of powder for a clean white
shirt."

"Scum, Scum," said Rummage, pecking at

him. "Have you ever listened to the words?"

Scum pulled his head out from under his wing and scowled at her.

"Of course I have. Why do you think I'm hiding?"

"No I mean *really* listened. Take this lot."

The flock were cawing cheerfully into the final "*Soapy Snow*" chorus, swinging their big black beaks from side to side in time with the tune.

"*Do we want to be dirty and afraid of the light?*" they sang,

"*Of course not! We want to be whiter than white!*"

"Do you?" asked Rummage.

"Do I what?" grumbled Scum.

"Do you want to be whiter than white? I don't."

"Of course not, silly! No crow would want to be white."

"So why are they singing it?"

"Huh?"

"Why've *we* been singing it?"

Scum shook his head. "I see what you mean. And I don't know why, except that it makes a change from caw."

The rooftop crowd continued relentlessly. "*Crunchy crisps*," they sang.

"The trouble is I'm hungry," groaned Scum. "I'm ravenous through and through and inside out and I can't think about anything when I'm hungry."

"I'm hungry too," said Rummage. "And so are they. Just look at them. They're starving to death but they don't seem to have noticed."

It was true. All the crows were looking half starved. Their feathers had lost their deep-black shine and their eyes, when they opened them enough to see, were grey and dull. If they hadn't been squashed up so close together and almost glued on with their own droppings, they'd have fallen off the roof. Even Rawk had lost his sleek profile. Now he looked more like a moth-eaten scarecrow than the pride of the flock.

"Cheese 'n' onion!"

"Prawn cocktail," they croaked blearily.

Scum groaned again. Suddenly he felt desperate.

"CRISPS ARE MUCK!" he shouted up at them.

"Cat food's yuk!" cawed Rummage, quick as a flash.

Scum looked at her with interest.

"That rhymes," he said. "How d'you do it?"

"It's easy," answered Rummage, "just make it up. You try."

Scum thought for a moment:

"Crisps are muck. Cat food's yuk," he muttered and then, *"Chicken Chasseur just gets stuck!"* he shouted.

"Yeah! Slugs and worms and garbage pie," sang Rummage.

"That's what you need to make you fly," answered Scum, and they both rolled around the gutter laughing and cawing fit to bust.

"That's good! I like it," said Scum. "We

don't have to sing *their* words… *'Slugs and worms and garbage pie,'*"

But the other crows were not amused. They shouted and cawed and screeched at Scum and Rummage.

"Silence!"

"We can't hear a thing with you making that racket."

"Behave yourselves!"

"Young crows should be seen and not heard."

Scum and Rummage looked at each other.

"I want some fun," said Rummage.

"*Ooh slugs and worms and…* I want some food!" said Scum.

They slapped wings.

"Time to fly!" they cawed.

And, hopping off the edge of the gutter, Scum and Rummage fell on to the wind and glided down towards Mrs Cox's backyard.

Chapter 6

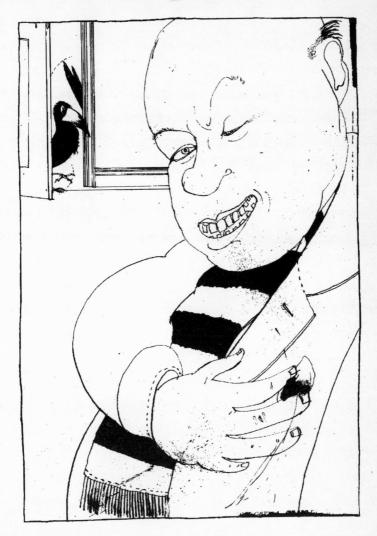

Mrs Cox

Mrs Cox's backyard was the nearest place for a quick snack. But with so many birds anxious not to miss a second of telly time, the supplies of easy food soon ran out. When Mrs Cox put her bin bag out on a Monday it was torn to shreds within minutes and the contents scattered and scoffed. Today was Friday. The place was a mess. All Scum and Rummage could find was a few empty tins and some torn pieces of Christmas wrapping paper.

They didn't mind. They weren't in any hurry to go back to the roof. Reminding themselves of the old tricks, they dug out some fresh worms and beetles hiding in the border and, when they'd snacked on these, they settled down to preen themselves in the winter sunshine.

"So where are we going to find it?" said Scum.

"What?" said Rummage.

"Fun. And food of course."

Rummage put her head on one side and stared at Mrs Cox's back door for a moment or two.

"That could be fun," she said.

"What?"

"That… I dare you!"

"Dare me what?"

"Dare you to go through the cat flap into the house."

"Are you mad?"

"Chicken," said Rummage.

"I'm crow, all crow!" squawked Scum indignantly. "Who are you calling chicken?"

"You," said Rummage. And she hopped through the cat flap herself.

As her eyes got used to the gloom, Rummage found herself in a narrow back scullery. Beyond it, through a slightly open door, she could see the light and hear the burble of the television from Mrs Cox's living room. There were two coats hanging up and a pair of outdoor shoes, some shelves with jars and packets on them, a plastic dustbin and, on a piece of newspaper beside the doormat, a bowl of half-eaten cat food and a saucer of milk. Rummage dipped her beak into the milk and drank.

The cat flap creaked. Scum looked in nervously.

"You're crazy!" he hissed, hopping in after her.

Rummage ignored him. She took one sniff of the cat food and ignored that too. Then she headed for the dustbin and, levering the lid up with her beak, pulled out a long string of juicy potato peel.

"That looks good!" whispered Scum, hopping after her and sticking his head into the bin too.

The lid slid off and clattered on to the floor.

"YIAAAOOW!" came a hunter's snarl from Fluffikins in the other room.

"Be quiet, you silly boy," said Mrs Cox, holding him firmly in her lap as she brushed his fur. "Lie down and stop fussing."

Scum was shaking so much he could hardly swallow his piece of potato peel but Rummage soon got over the fright.

"*Stay cool. The cat's a fool,*" she chirped, hopping across the floor and up on to one of the shelves. "*Don't disappear, we've got treasure here!*" she added and pecked at the side of a large paper bag with a picture of a budgerigar on it.

A stream of golden bird seed poured out on to the floor.

"How about that?" she said with satisfaction.

"Stone the crows!" gasped Scum.

They were so busy eating that they didn't hear Bernard arrive. The first they knew of it was when they heard him talking to Mrs Cox in the other room. Rummage tiptoed over to the door and peered through a gap in the hinge side. She beckoned to Scum with her wing.

Bernard was wiping bird muck off his spectacles.

"This is a nice surprise!" Mrs Cox was saying. "What are you doing here in the middle of the afternoon? Is everything all right at work, dear?"

Fluffikins yowled and spat in her firm grip. "Hush, Puss, hush," she said.

"I had some good news so I thought I'd pop over straight away to let you know," said Bernard turning his attention to his spattered coat sleeve. "I've heard from the Pest Control Department at last. They're making a special trip to come and sort out your bird problem tomorrow." He beamed at her. "They're bringing poison feed, anti-bird gel for the gutters and chimney pots and they'll net and kill as many as they can reach. Isn't that good news?" He brushed his hands off with a smug smile.

Behind the door Scum and Rummage looked at each other in horror.

"Oh, Bernard. You shouldn't have gone to

so much trouble, really you shouldn't," Mrs Cox was saying. "Eh, Timmy?" She whistled at the blue budgie who was watching the TV screen.

Bernard looked up from picking the bird-droppings off his sleeve.

"It's no trouble, Mother. It's a matter of principle," he said pompously. "A matter of public hygiene, that's what it is. They're pests! They're vermin! I've never seen anything like it. They're everywhere!" He was getting quite worked up.

"Yes, dear. Of course, dear," said Mrs Cox soothingly and changed the subject. "I don't suppose you managed to get hold of the telly man at all?" she asked. "It's the "One in a Million" final tonight and I had hoped… The picture gets ever so fuzzy you know."

Bernard looked smug again. "As a matter of fact I did. He's coming tomorrow afternoon when the pest control people have been."

Mrs Cox sighed. "You're a good boy Bernard. I don't know what I'd do without you." Fluffikins scratched and struggled. "And I wish I knew what was the matter with this silly cat."

"Perhaps you should just let him go for a while," said Bernard impatiently.

"Yes, dear," said Mrs Cox, and did.

Something rattled in the back door, but by the time the mighty Fluffikins had streaked across the living room floor and through the door into the scullery there was not a sign of Scum and Rummage anywhere, just the cat flap swinging and an ever-growing pile of bird seed on the floor.

Chapter 7

Bad News

Scum and Rummage fled back to the rooftop, cawing the bad news. But not one of the flock would listen. The "One in a Million" final was only hours away and the crows could think of nothing else. Who was going to win? Would it be the Grunge Granny of Peckham Rye or Wicked Rick and the Tweenies, Frizzy Lizzie the Singing Bee or Shockarocka?

The crows were much too busy keeping their places on the roof to listen to Scum and Rummage's breathless news of poison and anti-bird gel, nets and Pest Control officers. They told them off for interrupting important discussions with their silly stories. Even Rawk behaved as if he was deaf. He was concentrating on keeping his eyes shut and his wings still in order to pass on a clear picture to the rest of the flock.

"What are we going to do?" said
Rummage, landing on the gutter of the house
opposite.

"Do?" said Scum. "What can we do? If
they won't listen to us there's nothing we *can*
do. Let them stew."

Rummage was shocked.

"What's the matter with you? Birds of a
feather stick together, remember?"

"Well *they're* not sticking with *us* are they?"
he argued. "The only thing they're sticking to
is the blasted pictures."

Rummage put her head on one side and
looked thoughtful.

"That's right," she said.

"The way they are now, we'd have to be on
the TV before they'd take any notice of us."
Scum went on gloomily.

"That's RIGHT!" squeaked Rummage.
She hopped up and down on the edge of the
gutter. "BRILLIANT! You're brilliant Scum.
Why didn't I think of that? We'll go on TV!"

Rummage took off and looped the loop.

"*TV tee hee,*" she sang. "*That's no problem for Scum and me!* No problem at all!"

Scum perched on the edge of the gutter and watched her.

"It *IS* a problem," he shouted. "It's several problems. Like we don't even know where the blasted pictures come from, where the TV programmes are made."

"Ah ha," cawed Rummage zooming close past his head, "*We* don't… But Doom does."

"Doom?"

"Yes, Doom! Don't you remember? All those endless stories about his granny and how she used to take him there when he was just a fledgling and how she had a special arrangement with the rubbish collectors at the television building. Yes. Doom could show us the way!"

"Hmph," said Scum, ducking as she skimmed past on the other side. "Even if we could find the place, when have you ever seen a crow on TV? I suppose you think we can just walk on with a news bulletin? *Here is a news flash. Calling all crows, all crows: the pest control team will be arriving to exterminate the flock at 23 Blount Street tomorrow morning. Evacuate! Evacuate!*" Scum sighed in exasperation, "There's not a hope! Not a chance in a million."

Rummage did one last spectacular double somersault in the air and swooped back to the gutter to land beak to beak with Scum.

"But that's exactly it," she said. "Don't you see? 'One in a Million'! If Frizzy Lizzie the Singing Bee can get into the final, then so can we!"

It was a long time since the young crows had been to the park. The bare winter trees looked strange without their usual decoration of crows and bird-droppings but it was all the easier to find Doom. There he was, sitting in the big beech tree, a bit greyer round the beak, a bit stiffer and quite a lot fatter now he didn't have to share the scraps in the park bins with anyone else.

Doom was pleased to see them. It was a lonely business sitting the winter out on his own, and, if the truth had been told, the old crow was a bit bored too, though he was much too proud to admit it. He listened gravely to Scum and Rummage, shaking his head when they came to the bit about the Pest Control Officer and how the others wouldn't listen. But when they explained their plan, his shaking turned to nodding and a twinkle came into his beady old eyes.

"I haven't been over to the television building for years and years," he mused. "Show you? Of course I'll show you. I'll be glad of the outing. Now my old grandma, she loved music you know, she used to go over there all the time, and then there were these lorries she'd tell us about, she'd say... "

Rummage clutched her head in her wings and dropped off the branch she was sitting on.

"Is something the matter?" asked Doom. "You're in a bit of a hurry? Oh! Well. We'd better go then."

Old Doom flew agonizingly slowly. Scum and Rummage tumbled and rolled round and above and below him as he went, in a frenzy of impatience. Away from Blount Street he flew, across the park and over the railway lines, high above row after row of close-packed houses, over supermarkets and car parks, streets and traffic jams, offices, factories and church spires, on towards the west of the city. And still he flew. The light faded out of the sky and below them the street lamps came on.

"It's not far now," he said at last, "just past those office blocks, next to the canal. D'you see it? That concrete building with the floodlights?" He sighed and slowed down even more. "Oh my grandma used to love it over there. The stories she used to tell us chicks, about the TV stars and the presenters and the scraps and the stuff they used to throw away! But that was a long time ago."

Scum looped the loop impatiently, "Hurry!" he said. "There's no time to waste!"

But Doom had already gone, dropping down towards the TV building like a great black stone.

They found him in the central yard of the television building, hiding in the shadows of a low wall. "This is it!" he cawed quietly. Scum and Rummage looked round nervously. In front of them some stagehands in blue overalls were busy moving pieces of stage scenery out of a lorry and into the building through huge hangar doors. But Doom wasn't looking at them. He was staring hard towards the entrance of the yard. Scum and Rummage followed his gaze and saw four large open-topped lorries waiting in a row. A fifth was reversing up the yard towards a row of huge wheelie bins crammed with food and kitchen scraps waiting by the back door of the canteen.

"Bless my beak!" whispered Doom, his old eyes round as saucers. "If it isn't the garbage convoy my granny told me about all those years ago! And just about to load up! This is our chance for the feast of a lifetime! Come on!" and he started to hop towards the bins. Rummage blocked his way. "There isn't time!" she hissed urgently. "We must save the others! The show will be starting any minute and you've got to tell us how to get into this place."

Reluctantly Doom tore his eyes away from the reversing truck and nodded towards the hangar doors ahead of them. "That's the way," he sighed.

"Come on then," said Scum and Rummage, positioning themselves one on either side of him.

The three crows hopped quickly across the yard and in through the doors. They found themselves in a street of wooden house fronts.

"Well, look at that! It's Abdication Street!" said Scum, "from the series. And I always thought it was a real street."

He hopped up on to one of the windowsills and looked through a window to the empty space behind. "What a cheat! Just wait till I tell the others about this!"

Rummage had run out of patience. "Hurry up!" she squawked.

There was an answering shout from one of the stagehands.

"'Ere! What are those big birds doing here?"

"Don't know," answered another, "they must have escaped from the Zoo Show. You try and catch them. I'll give the guards a call."

A big woman in overalls advanced towards them with her arms spread wide. Nearer and nearer she came. The crows backed away, back and back until they found themselves in a corner and couldn't back any further. High walls stretched up behind them and the woman was closing in.

"Break out!" screeched Scum, making a dash through her legs. Doom and Rummage flew up over her head and together they fled across the set and into an empty corridor beyond in a flurry of feathers. Behind them they could hear voices shouting and footsteps racing after them.

"Hurry!" cawed Rummage. "We've got to find somewhere to hide!" and then, seeing a door that wasn't quite closed, "Quick! In here!"

They slipped through the crack, pushed the door shut and waited breathlessly until the voices passed them by.

They were in a small office. It had two chairs, a desk covered with papers, a filing cabinet, a mirror and, on the other side of the room, a second door with a baseball cap hanging on it.

"Disguise," said Scum flying up and unhooking it, "that's just what we need," and he dropped it on to Doom's head. "And look, there are two pairs of sunglasses on top of the filing cabinet. They'll do for you and me. Come on Rummage, lend me a claw!"

The voices were coming back along the corridor now. There was no time to waste. But where could they go? Rummage had her ear to the second door.

"Listen!" she hissed. On the other side they could hear the sound of an orchestra warming up and starting to play.

"It's one of the 'One in a Million tunes'!" squeaked Rummage. "We've made it! We're there!"

She swivelled the baseball cap round back to front on Doom's head.

"What do you reckon?" she asked.

"Terrific!" said Scum.

"Now are you sure you can remember what to do?" she asked.

"Of course!"

"Caw."

"Then let's go!"

Rummage hopped up and swung on the door handle, Scum and Doom levered at the edge of the door with their beaks and their claws and slowly, very slowly, the door swung open.

Chapter 8

Crow Talk

The three crows were dazzled by a great blaze of light. They were on the edge of a gold-draped stage. In front of them, facing row after row of red plush seats, Dilly and the Dweamers were just finishing their version of "Doo-bee doo-bee-doo". The people in the seats were clapping. The powerful television lights were gleaming. Two huge cameras on wheels were pointing at the stage and another at the audience. And Fat Henry, the host of "One in a Million", dressed in a gold sequinned jacket and flanked by two girls in bathing costumes, was waving the Dweamers off the stage in a cloud of chiffon and perfume.

"And now…" drawled Fat Henry. "We have a surprise for you."

With a well-practised smile at the nearest

camera, he stretched out his hand and swivelled round on his shiny shoes towards the stage... And there, standing in the spotlight, were ... not Shockarocka, not Wicked Rick and the Tweenies as he'd expected but three large black crows, two in dark glasses and one in a back-to-front baseball cap.

For a moment Fat Henry faltered. His beaming smile froze. He looked puzzled. But Scum and Doom didn't give him time to think. Together they set up a rhythmic

Caaw Caw
Caaw Caw

and clapped their wings while Rummage, hopping up to the lens of the camera and staring straight into it, began to sing.

Crow talk, she sang
Slow talk.
It's time to get some rhythm on this show
   talk.
– Caw.
Don't make a fuss.

Just listen to us.
It's time for some get up and go talk!
– Caw.

The members of the orchestra, who had been looking at the stage in some confusion, had got the idea by this time. One by one they started to join in with the rhythm. The audience thought it was all part of the plan for the show. They joined in too. Feet started tapping. Heads started wagging. Hands were clapping along in no time and, as Doom kept the beat going, Scum took over the lead.

Are you all of a heap? he sang.
Half asleep?
– Caw.
Glued to the telly by the tip of your beak?
Do you need a snack?
Have your wings gone slack?
Stiff legs? Dull eyes? Creaking back?
Then it's crow talk you need.
Show talk.
Get up off that roof and don't be slow talk.
Can't you see?

It's Doom, Rummage and me.
And we're warning you of danger, don't you
know.
– Caw.

At 23 Blount Street Mrs Cox peered at the fuzzy picture on the screen with a puzzled expression and started leafing through the TV magazine.

"I thought I knew all the contestants," she muttered, "but I'm sure I haven't seen these before. Who can they be?"

Fluffikins was not listening. He couldn't take his eyes off the screen, his fur was standing on end and his tail was twitching.

High above them on the slopes of the roof the half-hypnotized crows shifted restlessly in the dark and cawed to each other:

"Did you hear that?"

"Can you see what I see?"

"Can it really be?!"

"Crows? On TV?"

"Yes, crows! Crows!!"

"And not just any crows. They say they're Doom and Rummage!"

"What? Looking like that?"

"Yes! I'd know them anywhere."

"Ssssh! She's talking to us!! Listen!!!"

Calling Soot and Smut,
  – Caw.
Rawk and Squawk.
  – Caw.
Scab, Scar, Leatherlegs,
the Blount Street flock.
It's time to fly!
Get on up in that sky,
because the Pest Man's a-coming
and you're all gonna DIE!
  – Caw.
Get on the move!
  – Caw.
Get out and groove!
You've been sitting there so long
you've just got to prove
that you ain't beat yet

or we're ready to bet
that you're gonna be caught
in that Pest Man's net.
"Altogether now," croaked Doom.
Crow talk.
— Caw.
Slow talk.
Hear the warning! Watch out!
Danger! Time to go talk.
Let's get back to the park
and the trees and the dark
and the best crow life that we know!
Caaaaaaw!

The applause was like thunder. The audience
were on their feet shouting and cheering and
Fat Henry the host was wreathed in smiles as
Scum and Rawk and Rummage bowed and
bowed. But on the other side of the city
turmoil had broken out on the roof of 23
Blount Street in a flurry of wings and beaks
and argument.

Chapter 9

Doom

··

The three crows didn't stay to find out their
score. Despite Doom's protests they didn't
even stay to see what had happened to the
famous rubbish trucks. Dropping the
sunglasses and the baseball cap in a corner,
they fled from the television building as fast
as they could and didn't stop until they were
safely up in the air.

Scum and Rummage were still full of
excitement as they headed back across the
dark city. They turned somersaults in the air
and swooped and played as they flew.

"What do you reckon then?" gloated Scum.

"You were brilliant!" cawed Rummage.

"So were you!"

"And those *caaw caws*, Doom ... wicked!"

"But did it work? That's what I want to
know," said Scum. "Were the others watching?

Did they get the message? Did they believe us?"

"The only thing that really matters is that they leave that roof tonight," said Rummage. "If they once settle down to sleep there, they've had it ... the Pest Control people will get them in the morning, as sure as slugs are slugs. "We've just got to get back to 23 Blount Street as fast as possible and make sure that they go!"

The two young crows flapped on through the dark, watching the lights of the cars gleaming below them, like necklaces of red and white beads.

"What do *you* think, Doom?" asked Rummage at last.

The grizzled old crow had been silent all the way. Now it took him a while to answer.

"Pity about those rubbish trucks," he croaked at last, "...enough there to feed us all for a week." There was another long pause.

"Doom?" said Scum. "Are you all right?"

"... Bit puffed," came the answer. "Haven't been so far for a while."

It was then Rummage realized that all was not well. Doom was flagging, his wing beats were getting slower and slower. His beak was hanging open and his breath was coming in gasps.

"I think we'd better look for somewhere to rest," she cawed across to Scum.

"Not safe..." gasped Doom. "Must get back... Save the others... Hurry... Leave me!"

Rummage and Scum looked at each other.

"Leave you! Of course we're not going to leave you. Not until we've got you back to the park anyway, don't you worry." But Scum didn't feel as sure as he sounded.

Doom was losing height now, his eyes were misting over, his breathing was getting faster and shallower. They were so low they could hear the traffic roaring. Scum flew close beside him.

"Come on, Doom," he said. "You can make it!" and he started to sing softly.

"No talk.

Take it slow.
I'm beside you and there's
Rummage just below.
We'll soon be there,
just keep riding the air,
flap your wings and let it flow.
Caw."

Slower and slower went Doom. The railway lines appeared and up ahead Scum and Rummage could see the dark patch which was the park and safety. But the old crow could scarcely move any more. It was as if he was falling asleep or worse…

Scum and Rummage sang louder and more desperately trying to will him on.

"*Doom's a cool crow,*
Don't you know.
He took us to the telly,
got us on the show."

Beat by painful beat Doom flew on until, just as they reached the motorway, his strength gave out altogether. He seemed to freeze. His wings failed and he began to fall, half lurching, half gliding down towards the shadowy traffic below. Scum and Rummage tried desperately to support him, but the old grey crow was too heavy for them. They watched helplessly as he dropped away.

"NOOOOOOOOOO!" screamed Rummage into the night.

"DOOOOOM!" cawed Scum.

And just then, as if from nowhere, a crowd of mangy black shadows appeared out of the darkness cawing their names. It was the flock!

Scum and Rummage had never been so glad to see their brothers and sisters, aunts and uncles, cousins and friends in all their lives. They were caught up in a swirl of wings and a chorus of cawing, greeting, asking, thanking. But there was no time for celebration. All Scum and Rummage could manage was:

"Doom! Doom!"

"He's fallen… Down there! On to the motorway!"

"We've got to go after him!"

Diving towards the road, Scum left Rummage to explain to the others as they struggled wearily after her.

It was late. The traffic on the motorway was thin. One or two fast cars swished by. An articulated lorry roared. Scum flew so low he could see every pebble on the road. He flew back the way they had come and on in the broad direction of the park. But Doom seemed to have vanished off the face of the earth.

Scum was almost in despair when he saw just ahead of him a row of five heavy lorries grinding their way slowly in the direction of the park. Suddenly he thought he heard something.

"Caaw! Down here!"

"Here! Scum!" called a faint, familiar voice.

Scum flew over the convoy of trucks. Over the fifth one. The fourth one. The third one. The voice called again, nearer this time, except that it had a strange muffled sound, like someone cawing with their beak full.

"*Winkles and ham!*" it sang,

"*Spaghetti and jam!*

Fill your belly,

lovely smelly rotten

tuna meringue!"

Scum flew lower and peered into the back of the first lorry.

"*Five kinds of peel,*" came the voice.

"*Here's a flock-sized meal,*

riding along on twelve big wheels."

There was Doom! He was lying back on the biggest load of garbage that Scum had ever seen, looking exhausted but triumphant. He flapped a wing feebly as Scum flew over.

"Down here," he cawed. "Just look at this!" And even in the darkness Scum could see the twinkle in his eye.

"*Crow talk.*

What a show!

Caw.

I've found granny's

garbage trucks from long ago.

Caw.
No need to fly
way up in the sky.
There's a feast
on the road down below!
Caw."

Suddenly Scum felt so hungry he could hardly move his wings. He soared up into the air, light with relief.

"OVER HERE!" he cawed back at the rest of the flock.

"IT'S ALL RIGHT! I'VE FOUND HIM! COME AND SEE!"

And with a spectacular treble loop-the-loop, he dived into the garbage truck, with Rummage and the rest of the flock in hot pursuit.

Chapter 10

Spring

The story of that night became a legend among the birds of the city.

How the ragged crows feasted! How they cawed! They emptied truck after truck of the great garbage convoy and then rode in comfort all the way back to the edge of the park and tumbled into the trees so full they could barely balance on their branches.

For weeks afterwards Scum and Rummage and Doom were celebrated from treetop to tower block throughout the city. Their songs and rhymes swept through the crow population like wildfire and passed into the caws of the flock to be handed down from beak to beak for generations to come. It was as if TV jingles had never existed.

The mangy, half-starved crows took some time to recover their strength but, bit by bit, fortified by their new source of food, their moth-eaten feathers were replaced by shiny new plumage and their bleary eyes grew bright again.

Spring was coming. The sun was getting warmer. Wild food was becoming plentiful as the grass started to grow and the world seemed as new as the young leaves on the trees.

"I can't understand what we saw in it all," said Rawk to Doom as they shared a particularly juicy worm one afternoon a few weeks later. "You were right. We should have listened to you. What could be nicer than this roost in the park? It all seems like a strange bad dream."

"No, no," said Doom. "Give the youngsters their due. I'd never have remembered my granny's garbage trucks if it hadn't been for them!"

Scum and Rummage were dare-diving from the top of the old beech tree.

"Like a dream? Nonsense!" said Scum as he dangled upside down from a very thin branch. "All that television was real all right."

Rummage came hurtling past him, wings closed, heading straight for the ground.

"You bet," she squawked as she levelled out only millimetres from disaster. "Do you ever wonder who won the final?"

Scum spread his shiny spring wing feathers and stretched one leg.

"Yes I wonder," he cawed back. "I also wonder if it's still there."

"What?" said Rummage. "The aerial? Don't be crazy!"

"Why shouldn't I? I found it in the first place and I never did get a proper turn. Besides," he stretched the other leg, "everyone needs a change now and then." And he turned away from the roost and flew off in the direction of Blount Street.

"Scum?" cawed Rummage, "Scum! But what about the gel and the nets and the poison? Hey, wait for me!"

The spring sun had brought both Mrs Cox

and her neighbour out into their yards. They were leaning over the wall chatting when Scum and Rummage arrived.

"Have you been having a bit of trouble with your telly?" asked Mrs Batra. "I saw the vans outside a week or two ago."

"Yes, the picture kept going all wobbly. Terrible it was. But my Bernard got it all sorted out for me. All new too!"

Mrs Cox pointed up towards the roof top, past the gutters, now covered in wire mesh, and the tiles slimy with anti-bird gel to where a shiny new aerial and a satellite dish were bolted to the brickwork of the chimney. Two crows were perched on the aerial, they were swinging and jumping on it, leaning this way and that, wiggling and wobbling, cawing and cackling.

"Oh look, they're back. I *am* glad," said Mrs Cox. "My Bernard would have the pest control people in. He never does anything by halves, my Bernard. But I was sorry really. I like seeing the birds."

She turned back to Mrs Batra.

"The funny thing was, I'm not sure there was really anything *wrong* with the old aerial. You see the picture seemed to come right by itself just the night before they fixed it. Right in the middle of the 'One in a Million' final would you believe? I was ever so pleased. Did you see it?"

"Of course!" smiled Mrs Batra. "Wasn't it exciting? And the winner!"

"Pretty as a picture wasn't she."

"Frizzy Lizzie the Singing Bee."

"Wonderful little thing!"

"And that song."

"To tell you the truth though," said Mrs Cox confidentially, "my favourites were the mystery guests. Weren't they marvellous? It's wonderful what they can do with make-up and special effects nowadays isn't it."

"Oh yes," said Mrs Batra. "They looked just like those crows to me."

Mrs Cox stared up at the rooftop thoughtfully.

But Scum and Rummage had given up trying to get pictures out of the new aerial and were chasing each other up over the rooftops and into the clouds in search of something new.

JIM'S WINTER
Kathy Henderson

Jim's bored with the cold, damp, grey weather. But when the snow falls, his winter really starts to hot up!

"Told with humour and touching reality, this is an enjoyable and satisfying story with lots of appeal for children in the junior age range."
The School Librarian

SECOND-TIME CHARLEY
Kathy Henderson

When Charley Wilkins goes to bed on Thursday night, he expects to wake up on Friday morning. Instead, he finds himself back at the day before yesterday! For Charley the past is just beginning, bringing with it the key to an old mystery that could save his family's future fortunes!

This is a fast-moving and highly entertaining story for fluent young readers.

THE DUMP GANG
Martin Waddell

It's mind v. muscle when the Dump Gang take on the Bonzos!

Macmillan, Bo-Jeddy and little Quinn are the Dump Gang. Their deadly enemies are the Bonzos – Ratso, Big Boots, Meatface and co. Then there's Josie Swab, who's not in either gang but can make mincemeat of them both! Read about their entertaining escapades in these tip-top stories.

"A fun read, told with Waddell's customary flair and panache. Packed full of enjoyable insults, slapstick humour and racy prose."
The Times Educational Supplement

"Waddell knows how to turn a deft tale that is identifiable, imaginative and funny."
Scotland on Sunday

MORE WALKER PAPERBACKS
For You to Enjoy

☐ 0-7445-4793-8   *Jim's Winter*
           by Kathy Henderson   £3.99

☐ 0-7445-5287-7   *Second-time Charley*
           by Kathy Henderson   £3.99

☐ 0-7445-7245-2   *The Dump Gang*
           by Martin Waddell   £3.99

☐ 0-7445-7243-6   *Bernard's Prize*
           by Dick Cate   £3.99

☐ 0-7445-7815-9   *Dear Poltergeist*
           by Linda Hoy   £3.99

☐ 0-7445-6932-X   *Haunted House Blues*
           by Theresa Tomlinson   £3.99

☐ 0-7445-7718-7   *Capture by Aliens!*
           by Eric Johns   £3.99

☐ 0-7445-7817-5   *The Stone that Grew*
           by Enid Richemont   £3.99

**Walker Paperbacks are available from most booksellers,
or by post from B.B.C.S., P.O. Box 941, Hull, North Humberside HU1 3YQ**

24 hour telephone credit card line 01482 224626

To order, send: Title, author, ISBN number and price for each book ordered, your full
name and address, cheque or postal order payable to BBCS for the total amount and allow
the following for postage and packing: UK and BFPO: £1.00 for the first book, and 50p
for each additional book to a maximum of £3.50. Overseas and Eire: £2.00 for the first
book, £1.00 for the second and 50p for each additional book.

Prices and availability are subject to change without notice.

Name   _____

Address   _____

          _____